RAPUNZEL

WRITTEN BY

THE BROTHERS GRIMM

RETOLD AND ILLUSTRATED BY

RACHEL ISADORA

G. P. PUTNAM'S SONS

For the Penguins . . .
Nancy, Cecilia, Marikka
and Sara

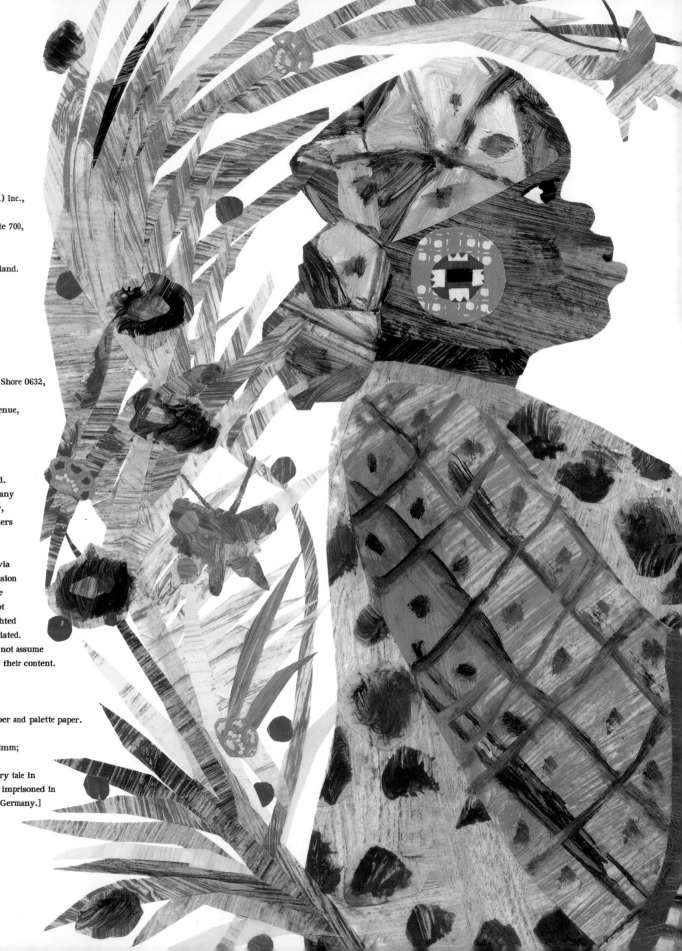

G. P. PUTNAM'S SONS
A division of Penguin Young Readers Group.
Published by The Penguin Group. Penguin Group (USA) Inc.,
375 Hudson Street, New York, NY 10014, U.S.A.
Penguin Group (Canada), 90 Eglinton Avenue East, Suite 700,
Toronto, Ontario M4P 2Y3, Canada
(a division of Pearson Penguin Canada Inc.).
Penguin Books Ltd, 80 Strand, London WC2R 0RL, England.
Penguin Ireland, 25 St. Stephen's Green,
Dublin 2, Ireland (a division of Penguin Books Ltd.).
Penguin Group (Australia), 250 Camberwell Road,
Camberwell, Victoria 3124, Australia
(a division of Pearson Australia Group Pty Ltd).
Penguin Books India Pvt Ltd, 11 Community Centre,
Panchsheel Park, New Delhi - 110 017, India.
Penguin Group (NZ), 67 Apollo Drive, Rosedale, North Shore 0632,
New Zealand (a division of Pearson New Zealand Ltd).
Penguin Books (South Africa) (Pty) Ltd, 24 Sturdee Avenue,
Rosebank, Johannesburg 2196, South Africa.
Penguin Books Ltd, Registered Offices: 80 Strand,
London WC2R 0RL, England.

Published simultaneously in Canada.
Manufactured in China.
Design by Marikka Tamura. Text set in Geist.
The illustrations were done with oil paints, printed paper and palette paper.
Library of Congress Cataloging-in-Publication Data
Isadora, Rachel. Rapunzel / written by the Brothers Grimm;
retold and illustrated by Rachel Isadora. p. cm.
Summary: Recasts in an African setting the familiar fairy tale in
which a beautiful girl with extraordinarily long hair is imprisoned in
a lonely tower by a witch. [1. Fairy tales. 2. Folklore—Germany.]
I. Grimm, Jacob, 1785–1863. II. Grimm, Wilhelm,
1786–1859. III. Rapunzel. English. IV. Title.
PZ8.I84Rap 2008   398.2—dc22 [E]   2007047104
ISBN 978-0-399-24772-9
10 9 8 7 6 5

Once there was a man
and a woman who longed
to have a baby. Finally
their wish was granted,
and the woman came
to be with child.

Next to their hut was a garden full of beautiful flowers and herbs. However, no one dared to go in it because it belonged to a wicked sorceress. One day the wife saw fresh rapunzel growing in the garden and had the greatest desire to eat some. With each passing day that she couldn't have any, her desire grew, and she became very ill.

Her husband asked, "What ails you, dear wife?"
"Oh," she answered, "if I do not get rapunzel, I shall surely die."

The man decided he must get some, no matter what. So that evening he climbed into the garden and quickly grabbed some.

The rapunzel tasted so good that now the wife wanted even more. Once again, the husband climbed into the garden.

And there, to his horror, stood the sorceress. "How dare you come into my garden and steal my rapunzel. You will pay for this!" she said.

The husband begged for mercy and explained that his wife would die if she did not have any.

"Well then, you can take the rapunzel, but you must give me the child your wife will soon bring into the world," she told him.

The man, in his terror, agreed.

When the child was born,
the sorceress appeared, named
the little girl Rapunzel and
took her away.

Rapunzel grew into
the most beautiful child
under the sun.

When Rapunzel turned twelve, the sorceress locked her in
a high tower that had neither a door nor stairs, but only a window
at the very top. When the sorceress wanted to enter, she stood
below and called out,

"Rapunzel, Rapunzel, let down your hair."

Rapunzel then wound her beautiful long hair around a hook and
let it fall to the ground below so the sorceress could climb up.

A few years later, a prince was riding by the tower
when he heard a song so lovely, he stopped to listen.
He saw Rapunzel in the window and fell in love with her.
He wanted to climb up but found no way to do so.

The prince returned every day to
hear Rapunzel's sweet song. One day
he saw the sorceress approach the tower.
He hid behind a tree to listen.

"Rapunzel, Rapunzel, let down your
hair," she called out.

He watched as the sorceress climbed
up to the tiny window.

The following day, the prince
went to the tower and called
as the sorceress had done,
    "Rapunzel, Rapunzel,
let down your hair."
    The hair fell down
and the prince
climbed up.

At first Rapunzel was frightened,
but then the prince spoke kindly and
explained that his heart had been touched
by her singing. Rapunzel lost her fear and
when he asked if she would take him for
her husband, she said yes. They said their
vows of marriage in the tower, and agreed
that the prince would visit every night,
for the sorceress came by day.

The sorceress did not find out
about the prince's visits until one day
Rapunzel said, "Please help me with
my dress—it seems to grow tighter every day."

"Why, you thankless girl," the sorceress cried,
realizing that Rapunzel was with child. "I thought I had
separated you from the world, but you have tricked me!"

She grabbed Rapunzel's hair and, snip-snap, cut it off!

Then she took poor Rapunzel into the wilderness,
where she left her all alone.

The sorceress returned to the tower and tied the cut-off hair to the hook of the window. When the prince came and called out, "Rapunzel, Rapunzel, let down your hair," she let down the hair. The prince climbed up, but instead of his beloved Rapunzel, he found the evil sorceress.

"Aha! You have come for your dearest, but you will never see her again."

The prince was so overcome with grief that he threw himself from the tower. He escaped with his life, but the thorns he fell upon blinded his eyes. He wandered through the wilderness for years, eating nothing but roots and berries, weeping over the loss of his beloved wife.

One day the prince heard a voice, and it seemed so familiar,
he went toward it. As he approached, Rapunzel recognized
him and threw her arms around his shoulders and wept.
Her tears fell on his eyes and he was no longer blind.

The prince led Rapunzel and their twins
to his kingdom, where they were received
with great joy and lived happily ever after.